P9-CFO-403

THIRD-GRADE DETECTIVES

The Puzzle of the Pretty Pink Handkerchief

By **GEORGE E. STANLEY**

Illustrated by **SALVATORE MURDOCCA**

ALADDIN · New York London Toronto Sydney New Delhi

*This book is dedicated to the wonderful
students in Mrs. Schlueter's third-grade class at
Lincoln Elementary School in Norman, Oklahoma. You're
great! Thanks for all your help.*

First Aladdin Paperbacks edition October 2000

Text copyright © 2000 by George E. Stanley
Illustrations copyright © 2000 by Salvatore Murdocca

Aladdin Paperbacks
An imprint of Simon & Schuster Children's Publishing Division
1230 Avenue of the Americas
New York, NY 10020

Designed by Steve Scott
The text for this book was set in 14-point Lino Letter.
Manufactured in the United States of America
12 14 16 18 20 19 17 15 13 11
0914 OFF
Library of Congress Cataloging-in-Publication Data
Stanley, George Edward.
The Puzzle of the Pretty Pink Handkerchief / by George Edward Stanley ;
illustrated by Sal Murdocca. — 1st Aladdin Paperbacks ed.
p.   cm. — (the third-grade detectives ; #2)
Summary: When he finds a clue to a mystery
in his tree house, Todd enlists the help
of his third-grade classmates to identify
the trespasser who had left it there.
ISBN-13: 978-0-689-82232-2 (pbk.)
ISBN-10: 0-689-82232-4 (pbk.)
[1. Schools—Fiction. 2. Mystery and detective stories.]
I. Murdocca, Sal, ill. II. Title.
III. Series: Stanley, George Edward.
The third-grade detectives ; #2.
PZ7.S78694Cj   1998
[Fic]—dc21   98-10576
CIP   AC

Chapter One

Todd Sloan's mother was in his room talking to him.

But Todd couldn't hear a word she was saying.

His ears were all stopped up.

It had started the night before.

His ears had suddenly closed up.

Then they popped open.

Then they closed up again.

Then they popped open again.

It was driving him crazy.

He had hardly slept at all last night.

"What? What? What?" Todd kept shouting to his mother. "I can't hear you!"

His mother stopped talking.

She gave him a tired look.

Suddenly, Todd's ears popped open.

"Ouch!" he cried.

It really hurt when that happened.

"You can't hear your teacher if your ears are all stopped up, Todd," his mother said. "I'm going to take you to the doctor this morning. He can clean them out."

"But they're not stopped up now, Mom. Honest," Todd said. "Anyway, I can't miss school today."

"Why not?" his mother asked.

"Mr. Merlin said he'd give us a new mystery to solve. What if he does it while I'm at the doctor's office?" Todd looked at her. "I promise! My ears will stay open now."

His mother shook her head in dismay. "I can't believe this. Ever since you started Mr. Merlin's class, you don't want to miss school. Well, finish getting dressed. I'll be back in a minute."

Todd's mother was right.

Mr. Merlin's third-grade class was special.

They were known as the Third-Grade Detectives.

They solved all kinds of mysteries.

It had all started because of Leon Dennis, too!

At the beginning of school, he had sent an unsigned letter to Amber Lee Johnson.

He had written her that she was the smartest girl in the world.

He hadn't thought anybody would know he had done it.

But Mr. Merlin had shown the class how to find out who it was.

Todd and Noelle Trocoderro had solved the mystery.

It was because of Leon's spit.

Mr. Merlin was really impressed by what Todd and Noelle and the rest of the class had done, too.

He'd said they were good enough to help the police solve crimes.

Suddenly, Todd's ears closed up again.

All he could hear was a ringing noise.

He knew he couldn't tell his mother, though.

She would take him to the doctor for sure.

Well, he'd just pretend that he could understand everything his mother said.

All of a sudden, Todd's right ear started to itch.

Todd wished he could crawl inside it and scratch all over.

He tried to ignore the itching.

But it wouldn't stop.

Todd rubbed his ear hard.

But that didn't seem to work, either.

So he took a tissue out of his pocket.

He stuck it just inside his ear.

He removed some earwax.

Finally, his right ear stopped itching.

But both ears were still closed up.

He couldn't hear anything for the ringing noise.

Todd tossed the tissue into the wastebasket.

Why did my ears have to be stopped up now? he wondered.

If he couldn't hear Mr. Merlin, he couldn't hear about the new mystery.

If he couldn't hear about the new mystery, he couldn't solve it.

Todd sighed.

He wished he knew how to read lips.

4

He had seen people on television do it.

They didn't have to hear people to know what they were saying.

Todd looked up.

His mother was standing at his door.

Her mouth was moving up and down.

Todd knew she was talking.

He watched her lips.

Suddenly, he knew what she was saying!

Your grandmother will take you to the doctor's after school.

Todd couldn't believe it.

He had actually read his mother's lips!

"Okay!" he said.

He grabbed his backpack.

Now it didn't matter if his ears were still stopped up.

He'd be able to read Mr. Merlin's lips.

He'd be able to solve the new mystery.

Chapter Two

Mr. Merlin was standing in front of the class.

His mouth was moving up and down.

But Todd's ears were still stopped up.

He couldn't hear anything Mr. Merlin was saying.

So he was trying to read Mr. Merlin's lips.

He wasn't having much luck.

Todd just hoped he could recognize the word "mystery" if Mr. Merlin said it.

Suddenly, his ears popped open.

"Ouch!" Todd cried.

Mr. Merlin stopped.

"Did somebody poke you, Todd?" he asked.

"No, sir," Todd replied. "My ears just popped open."

"Oh. Okay," Mr. Merlin said. "A lot of people in

school are having ear problems. There's so much pollen in the air."

Now Todd's left ear started to itch.

He thought he could feel something moving around inside it.

He took out a tissue.

He stuck it just inside his ear.

He removed some more earwax.

"Mr. Merlin!" Amber Lee cried. "Todd's sticking something inside his ear!"

Everyone in the class turned to look.

Todd was still holding the tissue in his hand.

"What are you doing now, Todd?" Mr. Merlin asked.

"I'm getting the earwax out of my ear," Todd said. He looked at Mr. Merlin. "Why do I have so much of it?"

"Everyone has earwax," Mr. Merlin said. "But some people have more if they're having problems with their ears."

"Why do we need earwax, anyway?" Noelle said. "It's so gross!"

"Well, earwax keeps the eardrums soft. If the eardrums weren't soft, we couldn't hear very

8

well," Mr. Merlin said. "Earwax also protects our ears. It keeps out dust and dirt and flying insects."

"I'm glad I have earwax," Amber Lee said. "I don't want anything flying around inside my head."

"Why not?" Leon said. "There's plenty of empty space!"

The class laughed.

Todd wondered what an insect would see if it ever got inside Amber Lee's head.

Suddenly, Todd's ears closed up again.

Oh, no! he thought. Now he couldn't take his eyes off of Mr. Merlin's lips!

But Mr. Merlin turned his back to the class.

He started writing spelling words on the board.

Maybe my ears will open up again before we start talking about the new mystery, Todd thought.

What if they didn't, though?

He'd have to be ready to read Mr. Merlin's lips.

But he needed to practice first.

He looked around the room.

He saw Amber Lee talking to Leon.

He watched Amber Lee's lips carefully.

He was sure she had said *police*.

He was sure she had said *principal,* too.

What is Amber Lee talking about? he wondered.

Had the police arrested their principal?

That would be awful.

He really liked Mrs. Jenkins.

His ears popped open.

"Ouch!" he cried.

Mr. Merlin didn't say anything this time.

He kept writing on the chalkboard.

"Did the police arrest Mrs. Jenkins?" Todd whispered to Noelle.

Across the aisle, Misty Goforth gasped. "Mr. Merlin! Mr. Merlin!" she cried. "Why did the police arrest Mrs. Jenkins?"

Mr. Merlin turned around. "What are you talking about, Misty?"

Misty pointed to Todd. "That's what he said."

Todd looked over at Amber Lee. "That's what Amber Lee told Leon."

"I did not!" Amber Lee said.

"Yes, you did!" Todd insisted. "I read your lips."

"Oh!" Amber Lee cried. She looked at Mr. Merlin. "Make him stop, Mr. Merlin! I don't want Todd reading my lips."

"Why are you trying to read people's lips, Todd?" Mr. Merlin asked.

"I only do it when my ears are stopped up," Todd said.

Mr. Merlin smiled. "Well, some people can read lips very well, Todd," he said. "But if you're not trained to do it, you can make mistakes."

"I didn't say the police arrested Mrs. Jenkins," Amber Lee said. "I said the police were in the principal's office this morning."

Mr. Merlin looked surprised.

"They were looking for Johnny Fowler," Leon said. "He played hooky from school again today."

Todd knew Johnny Fowler.

He was in the other third-grade class.

His father owned a bakery.

He made the best doughnuts in town.

Johnny helped him.

Todd had heard that Johnny played hooky a lot.

He wondered where Johnny was when he wasn't in school.

He thought about it for a minute.

If the police didn't know where Johnny was, maybe Mr. Merlin's Third-Grade Detectives could help them.

Todd was sure they could solve this mystery.

Chapter Three

Todd and Noelle were walking home from school.

They lived across the street from each other.

Todd's ears finally stayed open most of the day.

He was glad.

Now he didn't have to read anyone else's lips.

It was too easy to get into trouble doing that.

And now he didn't have to go to the doctor, either.

His mother had called him at school. His appointment had been cancelled. The doctor had gone home sick.

Todd wasn't glad the doctor was sick. But he was glad he didn't have to have his ears cleaned out today.

"I wonder if the police would let our class find out where Johnny goes when he plays hooky?" Noelle said. "That way they could work on other cases."

"They might. They already know how good we are at solving mysteries," Todd said. "Let's talk to Mr. Merlin about it tomorrow."

Suddenly, Todd's left ear started to itch again.

He could feel something else moving around inside it.

He pulled a tissue out of his pocket.

"You're not going to do that again, are you?" Noelle said.

"You're supposed to clean out your ears, Noelle," Todd said. "Haven't your parents taught you anything?"

Noelle put her hands on her hips. "Yes, they have!" she said. "They taught me that you're not supposed to clean out your ears in front of people!"

Todd grinned.

He looked right at Noelle.

He stuck the tissue inside his ear.

He pulled out some earwax.

"You are so gross!" Noelle said.

Todd started waving the tissue back and forth in front of her,

15

"Stop that!" Noelle cried.

Todd thrust the tissue at her.

"You'd better stop that," Noelle said. "I'm going to tell your grandmother if you don't."

They had reached Todd's house.

"I'm hungry," Todd said. "Do you want something to eat?"

"Sure," Noelle said.

Todd opened the side gate.

They headed for his back porch.

Todd's grandmother opened the door for them.

During the morning, she was a teacher's aide in the other third-grade class at his school.

Then she came to Todd's house right before Todd got home.

She stayed there until his parents came home from work.

"We're hungry, Grandma," Todd said. "Did you bake me some cookies last night?"

"Don't I always?" his grandmother said.

Todd grinned.

Noelle called her mother to tell her where she was.

Todd's grandmother poured two glasses of

milk and put the cookie platter in the center of the table.

"Can we eat in your tree house?" Noelle whispered.

"That's a great idea," Todd said. "I haven't been up there since last summer."

His grandmother put their milk in plastic cups.

She put their cookies in a plastic bag.

Then Todd and Noelle headed out the back door to the tree house.

Todd held the milk and cookies with one hand.

He used his other hand to climb up the rope ladder.

Noelle was right behind him.

When they were both inside the tree house, Todd said, "Where'd that come from?" He picked up a pink handkerchief.

"You probably left it here last summer," Noelle said.

"I don't use pink handkerchiefs, Noelle," Todd said. "Somebody else has been up here."

He held up the pink handkerchief to the light.

"Well, it's obviously been here for ages," Noelle said. "It's filthy."

"It looks like it has earwax on it," Todd said.

Noelle looked closely. "Hey! Maybe that'll tell us whose handkerchief it is."

"That's no clue. All earwax looks the same," Todd said. He pointed to a corner of the pink handkerchief. "Here's the clue. 'JPJ.' That's someone's initials."

"Who's JPJ?" Noelle asked.

"That's the mystery we have to solve," Todd said.

Todd and Noelle finished their milk and cookies.

Then Noelle went home.

Todd went to his room.

He put the pink handkerchief inside a plastic bag and laid it on top of his dresser.

He'd take it to school tomorrow.

He'd show it to Mr. Merlin.

The Third-Grade Detectives now had a new mystery to solve.

Who left the pink handkerchief in Todd's tree house?

Chapter Four

The next morning, Todd gave Mr. Merlin the plastic bag with the pink handkerchief in it.

"What's this?" Mr. Merlin asked.

"It's a new mystery," Todd said. "Someone has been in my tree house. I want to find out who."

Mr. Merlin opened the plastic bag.

He picked up a pencil.

He lifted out the pink handkerchief.

"It has some initials on it," Todd said. "If we can find the person whose name starts with those letters, then we can solve the mystery."

"It's also dirty," Mr. Merlin said.

"That's just earwax. It won't help us solve the mystery," Todd said. "Everyone has earwax."

The bell rang.

Everyone took their seats.

"Todd has a new mystery for us to solve," Mr. Merlin announced. "I'll let him tell you about it."

Todd came to the front of the room.

"Noelle and I found a pink handkerchief in my tree house," he said.

"The pink handkerchief has the initials JPJ on it.

"I want to find out who JPJ is."

"Only kids play in tree houses," Amber Lee said. "So I think it's someone who goes to our school."

"That certainly makes sense," Mr. Merlin said.

"It has to be a girl, too," Leon said.

"Why?" Mr. Merlin asked.

"Only a girl would use a pink handkerchief," Leon said.

Most of the class agreed.

"Okay. We need to find a *girl* at our school who has the initials JPJ," Todd said. "Then we'll know who's been in my tree house without my permission."

"I'm going to give you a secret code clue," Mr. Merlin said.

Mr. Merlin used to be a spy.

Todd knew Mr. Merlin liked to give them secret code clues to help them solve a mystery.

He said it made them think better.

Mr. Merlin turned around.

He started writing on the chalkboard.

He wrote:

20–8–5   3–12–21–5   9–19
9–14–19–9–4–5   23–8–1–20   9–19
9–14–19–9–4–5   20–8–5   5–1–18

Numbers! Todd thought. He'd never figure out that secret code clue.

But he didn't need a secret code clue, anyway.

All he had to do was be the first one to find a girl with the initials JPJ.

When the recess bell rang, Todd and Noelle hurried out the door.

"There's no girl in our class whose initials are JPJ," Noelle said. "I wonder which class she's in."

"That's what we have to find out," Todd said. "That's why we're detectives."

They started across the playground.

The other members of their class were looking for JPJ, too.

They were asking all the kids their names.

When the kids asked them why they wanted to know, they said they were just playing a game.

"Look!" Noelle said.

She pointed to a far corner of the playground.

Amber Lee was talking to a redheaded girl.

"Come on," Todd said. "We can't let her be the first one to solve my mystery!"

They ran across the playground.

"I found her. Jana Pauline Jones," Amber Lee said. "She's in the other third grade class."

"Hi," Jana said to Todd and Noelle.

Todd knew right away that something was wrong.

Both Amber Lee and Jana Pauline sounded sad.

"What's wrong?" Todd asked.

"I used to have a pink handkerchief. It had my initials on it," said Jana Pauline. "My grandmother gave it to me."

"What happened to it?" Noelle asked.

"I left it in my desk," Jana said. She sniffed. "Somebody stole it."

"Did you use it to clean out your ears?" Todd asked.

Jana gasped.

"I'd never do anything like that with my pretty handkerchiefs!" she said.

Amber Lee stamped her foot.

"It's not fair!" she said. "I thought we had this case solved."

Todd couldn't believe it.

He'd never thought of that.

He now knew who owned the handkerchief.

But it wasn't the same person who had left it in his tree house.

The bell to end recess rang.

Todd and Noelle walked slowly back to their classroom.

When everyone was seated, Mr. Merlin said, "Any luck?"

Todd told him what had happened.

"Well, has anyone solved the secret code clue yet?" Mr. Merlin asked.

No one had.

"Then I'll give you some rules," Mr. Merlin said.

Todd knew he had to listen carefully.

If he wanted to solve this mystery, he'd have to use the secret code clue after all.

"There are twenty–six letters in the alphabet," Mr. Merlin said. "Read them from left to right."

Chapter Five

Todd was disappointed.

He had hoped Mr. Merlin would give them a better clue.

Everyone knew there were twenty–six letters in the alphabet.

Everyone knew you read the letters from left to right, too.

But how will that help me solve the secret code clue? Todd wondered.

He looked over at Amber Lee.

She wasn't working on the secret code clue.

She was showing Leon a picture of Dr. Smiley.

Dr. Smiley was Mr. Merlin's friend.

She was a police scientist.

She used science to solve crimes.

Amber Lee was always telling people that she was going to be just like Dr. Smiley when she grew up.

Todd didn't think Amber Lee could ever be as good as Dr. Smiley.

He looked at the secret code clue again.

20–8–5   3–12–21–5   9–19
9–14–19–9–4–5   23–8–1–20   9–19
9–14–19–9–4–5   20–8–5   5–1–18

Was Mr. Merlin talking about which *number* each letter was?

Todd got out a sheet of notebook paper.

He wrote the numbers 1 through 26 in a column down the side.

Then, next to each number, he wrote a letter of the alphabet.

He started with *A* for 1.

He ended with *Z* for 26.

The first word of the secret code clue was 20–8–5.

Todd looked at the numbers with the alphabet on his piece of paper.

20 was *t*. 8 was *h*. 5 was *e*.

The!

Yes! he thought.

Now he knew how to solve it!

He matched the rest of the numbers of the secret code clue with the numbers on his piece of paper.

The secret code clue was: *The clue is inside what is inside the ear.*

What in the world does that mean? he wondered.

Suddenly, Todd's left ear started to itch again.

His ears weren't opening and closing anymore.

But he was still getting a lot of earwax out of them.

Todd was glad Mr. Merlin had told the class that earwax was a normal thing.

He didn't want people to think he was the only one who had a lot of it.

He took a tissue out of his pocket.

He stuck it just inside his ear.

He removed some of the earwax.

He looked at it for several seconds.

That's it! he thought.

Todd started waving his hand in the air.

"Mr. Merlin! Mr. Merlin!" he said. "I know what the secret code clue is!"

There was a lot of groaning in the room.

Several people said they had almost solved it, too.

"What does it say, Todd?" Mr. Merlin asked.

"The clue is inside what is inside the ear," Todd said.

"That's right," Mr. Merlin said. "Do you know what it means?"

Todd nodded.

He showed the class his tissue.

"This!" he said.

"Earwax can't be a clue," Amber Lee said. "Everybody has earwax."

"The clue is not the earwax," Todd said. "The clue is what's trapped *inside* the earwax!"

"Excellent!" Mr. Merlin said.

Just then, the lunch bell rang.

Chapter Six

It took Todd and Noelle several minutes to get their food trays.

The cooks had to make some more macaroni and cheese.

Now there were only two seats left at the tables where Mr. Merlin's class sat.

And they were across from Amber Lee and Leon.

"Why do we need to know what's inside *your* earwax?" Amber Lee demanded when Todd sat down in front of her. "That's not going to help us solve the mystery."

"It's not *my* earwax," Todd said. "It's the earwax on the pink handkerchief."

"We need to find out what's trapped inside it," Noelle said. "It may be something that will

tell us who was in Todd's tree house."

"Oh!" Amber Lee said. "I wish I had thought of that."

"How can we find out?" Leon asked.

Todd sighed. "I don't know," he said.

"I know!" Amber Lee said.

Todd looked at her. "How?"

"Dr. Smiley!"

"Do you think Mr. Merlin would take us back to the Police Laboratory?" Todd said.

"He won't have to do that. I'm having a meeting at Dr. Smiley's house after school today," Amber Lee said. "I can find out then."

Todd and Noelle gave her a puzzled look.

"I didn't know that," Todd said.

"Why didn't somebody tell us?" Noelle said.

"You're not invited," Amber Lee said.

"It's just for me.

"I'm going to talk to Dr. Smiley about starting a fan club.

"I want to be just like her when I grow up."

"That's not fair!" Noelle said.

"We like Dr. Smiley, too," Todd said.

"That doesn't make any difference," Amber

Lee said. "You can start your own fan club."

"Does Mr. Merlin know you're doing this?" Todd asked.

Amber Lee didn't say anything.

"I bet he doesn't," Noelle said. "He won't like it when he finds out."

Amber Lee looked at Leon.

"He won't mind," Leon said hurriedly.

"Yes, he will," Todd said. "He wants us all to cooperate."

"And you're not cooperating, Amber Lee," Noelle said.

"Okay! Okay!" Amber Lee said. "You can be members of the Dr. Smiley Fan Club."

Yes! Todd thought.

He wanted to be like Dr. Smiley when he grew up, too.

✦   ✦   ✦

When they got back to their classroom, Amber Lee said, "Mr. Merlin, may I make an announcement?"

"Yes, you may," Mr. Merlin said.

Amber Lee stood up.

"I'm starting a Dr. Smiley Fan Club," she said.

"I'm having the first meeting after school today.

"It'll be at Dr. Smiley's house.

"She's going to show me her home laboratory.

"She works there sometimes.

"I'm going to ask Dr. Smiley to help me find out what's trapped inside the earwax on Todd's pink handkerchief."

Oh, brother! Todd thought.

Amber Lee looked over at Mr. Merlin.

"I always try very hard to cooperate," she continued, "so I'll let anyone who wants to join my club."

"That is very nice of you, Amber Lee," Mr. Merlin said. He turned to the rest of the class. "You're all doing a great job trying to solve this mystery. Keep up the good work."

Noelle looked at Todd and rolled her eyes.

❀　❀　❀

For the rest of the day, they did schoolwork.

Mr. Merlin always made it interesting, but the day still seemed to drag by.

Todd could hardly wait until the last bell.

He wanted to get to Dr. Smiley's house.

He wanted to find out what was trapped inside the earwax on the pink handkerchief.

Chapter Seven

When the last bell rang, Todd hurried to the principal's office.

He telephoned his mother at work.

When she answered, he said, "We're going to Dr. Smiley's house, Mom.

"Mr. Merlin is walking there with us.

"We're having a meeting of the Dr. Smiley Fan Club.

"We're going to solve a mystery, too."

"Okay. Just call me when the meeting's over. I'll come pick you up," his mother said. "I'll also let your grandmother know that you won't be home."

"Thanks, Mom," Todd said.

He hurried out of the principal's office.

The rest of the class was waiting for him in the parking lot.

Mr. Merlin handed Todd the plastic bag with the pink handkerchief.

"You may give this to Dr. Smiley when we get to her house," he said.

Todd felt really important now.

Dr. Smiley lived three blocks from the school.

When they got there, Dr. Smiley was waiting for them on her front porch.

She was smiling.

Todd wondered what she would be doing if her name were Dr. Frowny.

The class followed Dr. Smiley into her house.

She led them to the kitchen.

"I thought we'd have a snack before we start the meeting," she said.

Todd saw a huge platter of cookies in the center of a table.

There was also a stack of plastic cups and three cartons of milk on the cabinet.

Dr. Smiley and Mr. Merlin poured the milk.

The class helped themselves to cookies.

They were store–bought.

Todd didn't think they were as good as his grandmother's.

But he still ate six of them.

Finally, everyone was full.

There weren't very many cookies left on the huge platter.

Dr. Smiley took everyone downstairs to the basement.

This was where she had her home laboratory.

"When do you work here?" Noelle asked.

"Sometimes I wake up in the middle of the night and think I have the answer to a problem at work," Dr. Smiley said. "I come down here then.

"I also use it if I'm tired of being in the office and want to get away.

"Sometimes, I use it for my personal research."

Amber Lee looked at Dr. Smiley. "Shall I call the meeting to order now?" she asked.

Dr. Smiley smiled. "That's fine with me, Amber Lee. Actually, I've never had a fan club before. I don't know exactly what we're supposed to do."

"I know," Amber Lee said. "I've been a member of a lot of fan clubs."

Everyone sat down on the floor.

Amber Lee stood next to a table.

"I'm calling this meeting to order," Amber Lee said. "Everyone but me has to quit talking."

She sure is bossy, Todd thought.

Amber Lee pulled a piece of paper out of her pocket.

"The first thing we need to do is elect officers," Amber Lee said. "I've come up with a slate of candidates."

Todd had no idea what Amber Lee was talking about.

He thought all they'd do was talk about the earwax on the pink handkerchief.

Amber Lee started reading.

"Amber Lee Johnson for president, vice president, secretary, and treasurer."

Amber Lee looked up.

"Do I hear a second?"

"Second!" Leon said.

"All in favor say 'Aye,'" Amber Lee said.

Amber Lee and Leon said, "Aye!"

The rest of the class just looked at each other.

"Now, as your president, vice president,

secretary, and treasurer," Amber Lee began, "the first thing I'd like to do is—"

Todd stood up. "How'd you get to be all those people, Amber Lee?"

Amber Lee gave him a hard look. "You're out of order, Todd Sloan. Sit down."

"No!" Todd said.

Mr. Merlin stood up.

"Maybe we should postpone the organization of the Dr. Smiley Fan Club until another time," he said.

"That might be a good idea," Dr. Smiley said. "I think we need to discuss this further."

Todd held up the plastic bag.

"Does that mean we can't find out what's trapped inside the earwax on the pink handkerchief?"

"No, I think that's one thing we can do today," Dr. Smiley said.

She took the plastic bag from Todd.

This is more like it, Todd thought.

In just a few minutes, he'd know who had been in his tree house without his permission.

Chapter Eight

"I'm glad you put the handkerchief in a plastic bag, Todd. That was the right thing to do," Dr. Smiley said. "You should always protect your evidence."

Todd smiled.

He was glad Dr. Smiley thought he was a good detective.

Dr. Smiley used some tweezers to lift the handkerchief out of the plastic bag.

Next, she carefully laid the handkerchief on a glass counter.

"Let's review what we know about this evidence," Dr. Smiley began.

"We know that two weeks ago someone stole this pink handkerchief out of Jana Pauline Jones's desk.

"We know that somehow it got earwax on it."

"Jana Pauline Jones didn't do it," Amber Lee said. She looked over at Todd. "She said she would never clean out her ears with one of her pretty handkerchiefs."

Dr. Smiley smiled.

The she looked closely at the earwax.

She touched it with a small knife.

"This earwax is still soft," she said.

"I'm sure it's not older than two weeks.

"Here's what I think happened.

"Whoever stole the pink handkerchief used it to clean out his or her ears.

"He or she probably did it in Todd's tree house.

"Since the pink handkerchief was now dirty, he or she must have decided to leave it there.

"He or she didn't realize it was evidence.

"This happens to a lot of criminals.

"They'll leave things at the scene of a crime that will help the police capture them."

Todd knew Dr. Smiley was talking about Leon.

Leon hadn't realized he was leaving behind his spit when he had sent Amber Lee a secret letter.

"Okay, detectives. Gather around the table," Dr. Smiley said. "Now we'll examine the earwax itself."

Everyone got as close to the table as possible.

"We'll take some of the earwax and put it on a microscope slide," Dr. Smiley continued.

She used a small knife to scrape off some of the earwax from the pink handkerchief.

She spread it in the center of the glass slide.

"That's just like spreading peanut butter on bread," Leon said.

"Oh, yuck!" Noelle said.

She moved away from Leon.

Next, Dr. Smiley put another glass slide on top of the first glass slide.

She held it up to the light.

"This should do nicely," she said.

She put the slide under the lens of the microscope.

She looked into the eyepiece.

Todd watched as she turned some knobs.

"This is interesting," Dr. Smiley said. "This is *very* interesting."

"What do you see?" Todd asked excitedly.

He moved closer to the microscope.

After all, he had found the pink handkerchief.

He should be the first one to find out what was trapped inside the earwax.

"Well, I see some things that you'd expect to see in earwax," Dr. Smiley said.

"I see particles of tree pollen.

"That's normal.

"All of the trees are starting to bud."

"How do you know that's what it is?" Noelle asked.

Dr. Smiley smiled. "I studied this in school. You have to remember what all kinds of things look like under the microscope."

Todd thought about that.

From now on, he'd try to remember everything that Mr. Merlin told them in class.

That way, he could do what Dr. Smiley did.

"What else do you see?" Amber Lee asked.

"I see some particles of dirt," Dr. Smiley said. "That's normal, too.

"But I also see something that not everybody has trapped in his or her earwax."

"What?" Todd asked.

"I see particles of flour dust," Dr. Smiley said.

She looked up from the microscope.

"I'm sure this earwax belonged to someone who's done some baking lately," she said.

Baking! Todd thought.

"The only person I know who bakes things is my grandmother," Todd whispered to Noelle.

Noelle gasped.

Did that mean his grandmother had stolen Jana Pauline Jones's handkerchief? Todd wondered.

Did that mean his grandmother had cleaned her ears with it?

Did that mean his grandmother had been up in his tree house?

Chapter Nine

Todd's mother was waiting for him in front of Dr. Smiley's house.

He got into the car.

He didn't say anything.

His mother drove away.

After a few minutes, his mother said, "Why are you so quiet, Todd? Is there anything wrong?"

Todd looked over at her.

"Do you think Grandma could have left that pink handkerchief in my tree house?" he said.

His mother started laughing.

"What in the world gave you that idea, Tood?" she asked.

"Dr. Smiley said whoever used the pink handkerchief to clean out his ears had baked something recently," Todd explained.

His mother looked puzzled.

"How did she know that?" she asked.

So Todd told her about earwax.

He explained how it traps particles from the air.

He explained how that keeps the particles from getting into the ear.

"The earwax on the pink handkerchief had particles of flour dust in it.

"Grandma is the only person I know who uses flour to bake things.

"She's also a teacher's aide in Jana Pauline Jones's class.

"She could have taken the pink handkerchief when Jana wasn't looking.

"Who else could it be?"

"Oh, now I understand why you might think that," his mother said.

"In fact, it shows a lot of thought on your part.

"But your grandmother couldn't have done it, Todd.

"First of all, she'd never take anything that wasn't hers.

"And her arthritis is too bad for her to climb

up that rope to get into your tree house.

"No, it has to be someone else who's been around flour dust.

"There are a lot of people in town who bake things."

They had reached their house.

His mother drove into the garage.

Todd was happy now.

He wanted to solve the mystery.

But he didn't want his grandmother to be the answer.

※   ※   ※

It was almost time for the bell to ring when Todd got to school the next day. He hurried into Mr. Merlin's room. He sat down in his desk.

"Grandma didn't do it. She has arthritis," he whispered to Noelle. "She can't climb up into my tree house. Someone else left the pink handkerchief there."

Noelle looked disappointed. "I thought we had solved the mystery," she whispered back.

"I did, too. But I'm glad Grandma didn't do it," Todd whispered. "I didn't want the police to arrest her."

Suddenly, Misty came rushing into the room.

She sat down.

She leaned over to Noelle.

"Guess what?" Misty whispered.

But she whispered so loud that Todd could hear every word.

"What?" Noelle whispered back.

"Johnny Fowler played hooky again today.

"His father was in the principal's office.

"Mrs. Jenkins was talking to him."

"How did you know it was Johnny's father?" Noelle asked.

"We buy our doughnuts from his bakery. I'd recognize him anywhere," Misty said. "He had flour dust all over his clothes."

Of course! Todd thought. *Why didn't I think of that?*

Now he knew who had stolen Jana Pauline Jones's pink handkerchief.

Now he knew who had left it in his tree house.

The only thing he had to do was prove it.

Chapter Ten

Todd looked at the big clock on the wall.

It was almost time for the last bell to ring.

He wanted to be by the door when it did.

He had to get home fast.

He got up from his desk.

He walked to the pencil sharpener.

He pretended to sharpen his pencil.

The bell rang.

Todd hurried out of the classroom.

He ran across the parking lot.

He ran down the sidewalk.

He turned the corner.

Up ahead, he saw Johnny Fowler coming out the side gate of his backyard.

Johnny started walking in the opposite direction.

"Johnny!" Todd shouted. "Wait for me!"

But Johnny kept walking.

"Johnny!" Todd shouted again.

But Johnny didn't stop walking.

He acts like he doesn't hear me, Todd thought.

Finally, Todd reached Johnny.

He touched him on the shoulder.

Johnny whirled around.

"What do you want?" he said.

"I want to talk to you," Todd said.

Johnny gave Todd a funny look. "What? What? I can't hear you!" he said.

His ears are stopped up just like mine were! Todd realized.

Suddenly, Johnny said, "Ouch!"

"What's wrong?" Todd asked.

"Nothing," Johnny said.

But he was rubbing his right ear.

"I know where you are when you're not in school," Todd said.

"Where?" Johnny said.

"You're in my tree house," Todd said.

"I am not," Johnny said.

He took a tissue out of his pocket.

He cleaned his right ear with it.

"I can prove it," Todd said.

"How?" Johnny asked.

"Let me have that tissue," Todd said.

Johnny looked down at the tissue in his hand.

"Why?" he said.

"It's evidence," Todd said.

Johnny thought about it for a minute.

Then he shrugged.

He handed Todd the tissue with his earwax on it.

"Come with me to Dr. Smiley's house," Todd said. "I'll show you how I know it's you."

Todd told his grandmother where they were going.

When they got to Dr. Smiley's house, she was just pulling into her driveway.

Todd introduced her to Johnny.

Then he gave Dr. Smiley the tissue Johnny had used to clean his ear.

"Can you show Johnny what's trapped inside his earwax?" he said.

Dr. Smiley looked at Johnny. "Is this all right with you?" she asked.

Johnny nodded.

Dr. Smiley took them down to her laboratory.

She scraped Johnny's earwax off the tissue.

She put it on a slide.

She looked at it under the microscope.

She turned to Johnny.

"You take a look," she said.

Johnny looked into the microscope.

"What are those funny-looking things I see?" he asked.

"They're particles of pollen, dirt, and flour dust," Dr. Smiley said.

"How did that stuff get into my earwax?" Johnny asked.

Todd explained it to him.

"Does that prove I was in Todd's tree house?" Johnny asked.

"No, Johnny," Dr. Smiley said. "It doesn't really prove that you were in the tree house."

Todd looked disappointed. "Why not?" he asked.

"Well, the flour dust in the earwax on the pink handkerchief is the same as the flour dust in the earwax on the tissue," Dr. Smiley explained.

"And I think the earwax on the pink handkerchief and the earwax on this tissue belong to the same person.

"But someone else besides Johnny could have put the pink handkerchief in the tree house.

"That's what a lawyer would say."

Todd and Dr. Smiley both looked at Johnny.

"I did it," Johnny said. "I left the pink handkerchief in Todd's tree house."

Todd thought Johnny seemed really happy that he'd been caught.

❋   ❋   ❋

The next morning at school, there was a meeting in Mrs. Jenkins's office.

Johnny Fowler was there.

So was his father.

So were Todd and Mr. Merlin.

Johnny wanted them to be there.

He told everyone what his problem was.

He didn't want to work so much at the bakery.

He wanted to do more things at school.

Johnny's father apologized.

He hadn't realized this.

Ever since Johnny's mother had died, Mr. Fowler hadn't done anything but work in the bakery.

He wanted Johnny to be there with him.

He had forgotten that Johnny needed to do other things.

"I want to be like the other kids at school, Dad," he said. He turned to Todd. "I want to do what you do."

Mr. Merlin had a solution.

He had already talked to Mrs. Jenkins about it.

He had already talked to Johnny's teacher, too.

Johnny would move to Mr. Merlin's class.

Johnny thought that was a wonderful idea.

Todd agreed.

"But you have to apologize to Jana Pauline Jones for taking her pink handkerchief," Mrs. Jenkins said.

Johnny looked embarrassed.

But he said, "I will."

Todd looked at him. "Do you like her? Is that

why you took her pink handkerchief?"

Johnny looked surprised. "No. I just needed something to clean my ears. Jana has so many pretty handkerchiefs, I didn't think she'd mind."

Todd laughed.

He was sure Johnny would fit right in with the rest of the Third-Grade Detectives.

Biters Beware!

Police scientists can solve crimes by looking at what's inside your ears. That's what Dr. Smiley did with earwax in the book you've just read. Police scientists can also solve crimes by looking at what's inside your mouth. Here's an experiment you can do at school (or with friends at home) to see how they do it.

1. Get four apples.

2. Choose four classmates and give each of them an apple. It's best to choose four class-mates whose teeth don't look the same.

3. Out of sight of the rest of the class, have each classmate take one bite out of his or her apple.

4. Line up the apples on a table so everyone can see the bite mark in each apple.

5. Can you tell who bit into which apple?

To match up the biters with the apples, all you have to do is ask each biter to open his or her mouth, and compare the person's teeth to the teeth marks on the apple.

Police scientists often solve crimes by com-paring a suspect's teeth with the teeth marks found on discarded food at the scene of a crime. Criminals who rob grocery stores or other places where food is sold will often eat part of a piece of fruit or pastry during a robbery and then leave it at the scene of a crime. Police scientists love to find this kind of evidence!